What a Story!

Magazine

Contributo

MultiSource™

SERIES
EDITORS
Margaret Iveson
Samuel Robinson

EDITORIAL
CONSULTANT
Alan Simpson

LITERATURE
CONSULTANT
Rivka Cranley

TEACHER
CONSULTANTS
Flora Miller
Eldred Barnes

COVER
ILLUSTRATION:
Phillip Singer

Dan Yashinsky, a Toronto storyteller, performs at schools, festivals, and theatres.

Zita Asbaghi is a freelance illustrator who lives in New York with her cat Suzie.

Paul Morin is an award-winning freelance illustrator from Calgary.

Prentice Hall Canada

Scarborough, Ontario
© 1993 Prentice-Hall
Canada Inc.
ALL RIGHTS RESERVED

No part of this book may
be reproduced in any form
without permission in
writing from the publisher.
Printed and bound in
Canada.
ISBN 0-13-020124-3

Gretchen Will Mayo writes, teaches, paints, and occasionally illustrates the books she has written.

Contents

Features

Departments

Young and old alike are captive to the natural human wish to be enchanted, to be swept away by a marvellous tale, and to find themselves exclaiming, "What a story!" To many people, a well-told story is an invitation to let the imagination run free, to live for a while in someone else's world, and to delight in human creativity.

Within the following pages, you will embark on a grand tour through places and times. Everywhere you go, you will find stories that have been sung, painted, danced, and cartooned, as well as those that have been told and written. Best of all, you will uncover a deep well of stories you may not have recognized: your own life!

> Stories are powerful. They are a journey and a joining.
> In a tale we meet new places, new people, new ideas.
> And they become *our* places, *our* people, *our* ideas.

JANE YOLEN

Today we live,
but by tomorrow today
will be a story. The whole
world, all human life,
is one long story.

Isaac Bashevis Singer

The fascinating thing about writing is that it's a way of transforming the things you've experienced; it's like being able to live twice.

Jacques Godbout

The traces of the storyteller

cling to the story the way

the handprints of the potter

cling to the clay vessel.

WALTER BENJAMIN

A Decade of Laughter

Montreal's tribute to the funny story • By Christopher Vaughn

Agents, managers and comedians laughed at, not with, Gilbert Rozon, Andy Nulman, and Bruce Hills during the early days of the now 10-year-old Just For Laughs Comedy Festival: "We'd tell people we were doing an international comedy festival in Montreal in July and we'd like them to come . . . and they would look at us like we were out of our minds," recalls Nulman.

They're still looking at the JFL group, but today it's with smiles of admiration and appreciation, for the festival has become the *ne plus ultra** of worldwide comedy gatherings. What started as a one-night French-language event has become a 10-day, multi-lingual indoor and outdoor festival that rivals Mardi Gras in its exuberance and the Cannes Film Festival in its importance to a performer's career. More than 250 acts from such countries as the United States, the United Kingdom, France, Australia, Canada, Japan, Russia, Sri Lanka, Kenya, and Zimbabwe journey to Montreal every summer to perform, schmooze, party and enjoy the world's biggest laughathon.

**ne plus ultra*: Height of excellence

Two jugglers perform for festival crowds on St. Denis Street.

And since laughter can be created from a multitude of formats, JFL features a plethora of talent-types. "It's a misconception to think of the festival as 'standup comedy' only," says Nulman, who started with Just For Laughs in 1985 and is now VP of the festival. "We also have performers like Michel Lauziere, who climbs into a balloon; Ennio Marchetto with his life-size paper dolls; Norbert Sinz, who does acrobatics in a wheel; and Mitchell Zeidwing, who plays piano with his nose."

Yes, but JFL is also known as the stomping ground, and often-times breaking ground, for the most talented standup comedians in the business.

"It's a lot of fun and games, but the main reason the festival works so well is because all the people associated with putting it on take it very seriously," says Marty Klein, president of APA (Agency for the Performing Arts), which started working with the festival during its third year after the agency's New York representative Lou Viola went up, phoned back and said, "These guys have got something here, they know what they're doing."

To keep it a hit year after year, Nulman and Hills work nonstop to get the best of the best. "We see well over 1200 acts worldwide to glean about 20 that will appear here at the festival," says Hills, the director of programming. "We watch tapes, go to clubs and theatres, and listen to the word of mouth generated by those who have attended the festival. We never know where we'll find something special, and we like to book it for a good balance—to have a certain number of ingredients that make the festival palatable. We make a sincere effort to bring in performers from all corners of the industry."

CHRISTOPHER VAUGHN *wrote this article for* The Hollywood Reporter *magazine.*

A Tell-Tale History

There has always been a job for the storyteller.

On blustery winter evenings when it's too cold to go outside, when dinner has been eaten and all the dishes put away, many North American families can be found gathered in their living rooms. There, a colourful glass box tells stories that average half an hour long, including commercials. Watching television is one modern descendant of a storytelling tradition that probably goes back to the very first human conversation.

Before the invention of the printing press, few stories were written down. In many cultures, professional storytellers earned their livings memorizing and reciting hundreds of stories. If they could find a position in royal courts, their tales provided a comfortable living. The *ollams,* or storytellers of thirteenth-century Celtic societies in northern Europe, were allowed to wear five colours in the court—only one less than royalty wore.

Being able to tell stories on demand required quite a mental library. Irish *shanachies,* who specialized in historical tales, usually drew from a memorized collection of over 150 stories. Tenth-century *skalds* of Norway and Iceland needed more than

their own assortment of stories, which were usually told in poetic form. Their job included relating heroic deeds they witnessed when they joined their lords in battle.

If professional storytellers failed to secure a royal position, they would travel throughout their country or even farther, telling stories for a price. As early as the fourth century, *minstrels*—including jugglers, musicians,

Matrioska dolls from Russia

and acrobats as well as storytellers—travelled all over Europe.

Other storytellers played music to enliven their tales, too, from the *minnesingers* of Germany and the *troubadours* of France to the *griots* of Senegal and Gambia. Some storytellers created their music on the spot while others used traditional tunes. Because many aboriginal cultures place

great importance on precise memorization, their stories have been preserved through numerous generations.

Visual aids also accompanied stories. In eastern Europe, nesting dolls, or *Matrioska,* symbolized the different generations mentioned in a story. Storytellers in Zaire and Angola carried a knotted rope with various tokens tied into it as a sort of menu. Listeners could choose an object and hear the corresponding story. The Incas of Peru also used a knotted cord, called the *quipu,* which they tied into configurations that would trigger their memories. Inuit storytellers sometimes drew with a knife in the snow or mud to illustrate their stories, while the Walberi in Australia made patterns in the sand.

Many of these oral traditions continue today in one form or another. As more people gain access to stories told through the media and through books, each culture has to decide whether and how to preserve the traditions of its oral storytellers.

By Dan Yashinsky

Who is a Storyteller?

Who are these people, the storytellers whose art has been practised throughout the ages? Our images of them range from the grandparent who tells stories at bedtime to the formal art of the epic singer. Between them is a continuum including the griot of Africa, the native North American elder, the Irish shanachie, the medieval minstrel. These tellers have always been the welcome guests at any gathering, from kitchens to campfires to royal courts. They have carried their stories on the high roads of the world, across seas and caravan routes. They have also remained at home, telling stories rooted in their own land. The storytellers have been people who in the practise of their craft found the occasion to relate tales and sing ballads. In fact, storytelling used to be so much a part of spinning and weaving that these became synonymous with the art of narration. To this day we still spin yarns and weave enchantment. . . .

When you begin to follow the storyteller's path you will quickly realize that everyone is a storyteller. Whether it be a reminiscence, a description of a person, a dramatic experience—everyone has a story to tell. It is up to you to listen!

DAN YASHINSKY *is a storyteller who was born in 1950. Since moving to Toronto in 1972, he has performed at schools, festivals, and theatres throughout North America and Europe.*

Stories have a way of cropping up ju

EV

"You'll never guess who placed first in the science fair. I was walking by the teacher's lounge this morning and . . ."

"I can't believe you never showed up last night! I waited for you guys in front of the theatre for forty minutes!"

"I'm telling you, if my little sister listens
...to one more of my phone conversations,
...'m going to make her swallow that
...hone! Last night . . ."

"I saw the scariest film the other night.
It was about all these rats that . . ."

"Do you have any idea
what will happen when
my parents see my
report card? They won't
let me leave the house
for two years!"

...ut everywhere. Try going through a day without telling one or hearing one.

...ey, lighten up! We almost got
...to a *major* car accident!. . ."

URBAN
Legends

BY RICHARD WOLKOMIR

When was the last time you heard a bizarre story that happened to "a friend of a friend"?

A woman's at the mall here last week, in that big discount store. She's looking at these rolled-up carpets from Asia. She sticks her hand into one to feel the thickness, and something pricks her finger. Then her hand swells up. Whole arm turns black. She falls on the floor dead.

So they unroll the carpet. Inside's a cobra, and about ten baby cobras.

A friend of mine told me. His cousin knows one of the salesclerks.

Hey, it's a jungle out there.

Just ask Jan Harold Brunvand—"Mr. Urban Legend." A University of Utah folklorist, Brunvand collects modern told-as-true tall tales like the cobra-in-the-carpet story. More come in every day from his informants around the world. They are weird whoppers we tell one another, believing them to be factual. Haunted airliners. A hundred-miles-per-gallon car the oil companies keep secret. How about that guy who stole a frozen chicken at the supermarket and hid it under his hat, then fainted in the checkout line because his brain froze? And did you hear about the guy who's eating fast-food fried chicken when he sees this scaly *rat's* tail sticking out of the batter?

The Pied Piper is still piping. But in our fiber-optic age he pipes an MTV tune. "These stories are like traditional legends—they reflect our concerns," says Brunvand. "But now we live in cities and drive cars."

In fact, many of the 500 or so modern legends that Brunvand has collected do involve cars. In previous eras, legends were often about specters, since ghosts bred like bunnies in the dark corners of candle-lit houses. Spooks still pop up, but now they ride in V-6's. That may be because cars offer a certain liberation. But freedom is scary. Out on that open highway, *anything* might happen.

Brunvand titled the first of his five urban legends books *The Vanishing Hitchhiker* (1981), after what he calls the classic automobile legend. Here's how it goes:

Well, this happened to one of my girl-friend's best friends and her father. They were driving along a country road on their way home from the cottage

If you think legends are a thing of the past, you may be in for a surprise. Maybe you've even told a few yourself!

when they saw a young girl hitchhiking. They stopped and picked her up and she got in the back seat. She told the girl and her father that she just lived in the house about five miles up the road. She didn't say anything after that but just turned to watch out the window. When the father saw the house, he drove up to it and turned around to tell the girl they had arrived—but she wasn't there! Both he and his daughter were really mystified and decided to knock on the door and tell the people what had happened.

They told them that they had once had a daughter who answered the

description of the girl they supposedly had picked up, but she had disappeared some years ago and had last been seen hitchhiking on this very road. Today would have been her birthday.

That version, says Brunvand, came from a Toronto teenager in 1973. But the story had begun going around North America at the turn of the century. The automobile motif had taken over by the 1930s. Usually the teller cites specific local streets where the driver picks up the spectral hitchhiker. Sometimes the ghost leaves a book or scarf in the car, which the bereaved

ILLUSTRATIONS BY KATHERINE STREETER

WORD
TALK

A **kissing cousin** is a relative close enough to be greeted with a kiss. The term became widely used in the South during the U.S. Civil War in reference to family members who shared the same political views. Today the term is most often used to describe similarity.

parents then identify as belonging to their lost daughter. Sometimes the driver spies the hitchhiker's photograph on the family piano, wearing the same party dress in which she died, and which she wore when he picked her up. Urban legends are kissing cousins of myths, fairy tales and rumors. Legends differ from rumors because the legends are stories, with a plot. And unlike myths and fairy tales, they are supposed to be current and true, events rooted in everyday reality that at least *could* happen. Like that woman given a microwave oven by her children. After bathing her poodle, she got the idea of drying it in the microwave—the poor poodle exploded! Other versions feature cats, parakeets and "one unfortunate turtle," says Brunvand. Before

microwave ovens appeared, the ill-fated pets met their doom in gas ovens or clothes dryers. Apparently our appliances make us uneasy, perhaps because technology mystifies us, a sort of scientific magic. People like to get scared. The legends, he adds, deliver a warning: "Watch out! This could happen to you!"

◆ ◆ ◆

"It was living folklore," says Brunvand. "When I started teaching at the University of Idaho, I discovered that students think folklore is always about somewhere else and another time—about getting to know your grandmother—and I wanted to show that it's also about getting to know yourself."

Real urban legends, he believes, are a group effort. "Most of them are communal. When a community circulates a piece of folklore, everyone participates in the creation, each performer adding something in his or her own style." Legends are continually recycled.

Clearly, urban legends run deep. And they keep coming, crying out for analysis. "I can't stop—as long as I open my mail and answer my phone, I'm going to get more stories," says Jan Brunvand. "And when a story's hot, suddenly it's all over the country, with allusions in newspapers and on talk shows." It's fascinating to watch the stories spread, he adds. "You're seeing the living tradition as it develops and changes."

> ## Urban legends are kissing cousins of myths, fairy tales, and rumors. Legends differ from rumors because legends are stories, with a plot.

RICHARD WOLKOMIR *was born in Catskill, New York, in 1943. He and his wife, Joyce, often work together on magazine articles, and recently published a book about endangered animals.*

EXPRESS
YOURSELF

Why do people seem to find bizarre stories more appealing if told they're true? Why are people so quick to believe an unbelievable story?

Bridges

A well-told story can link audience
to author in unexpected ways.

SURPRISE

The biggest
Surprise
On the library shelf
Is when you suddenly
Find yourself
Inside a book—
(The hidden you)
   You wonder how
   The author knew.

By Beverly McLoughland

BEVERLY MCLOUGHLAND
(born in 1946) has been writ-
ing poetry for seventeen years.
Her work has appeared in
magazines, anthologies, and
textbooks in several countries.

THE STORY-TELLER

He talked, and as he talked
Wallpaper came alive;
Suddenly ghosts walked,
And four doors were five;

Calendars ran backward,
And maps had mouths;
Ships went tackward
In a great drowse;

Trains climbed trees,
And soon dripped down
Like honey of bees
On the cold brick town.

He had wakened a worm
In the world's brain,
And nothing stood firm
Until day again.

By Mark Van Doren

MARK VAN DOREN *(1894–*
1972) was a U.S. poet, critic,
novelist, and teacher. Many
of his university students went
on to become famous poets.

ILLUSTRATION BY NANCY NIMOY

THE HUNTER AND Rainbow

Retold by Gretchen Will Mayo

What explanations have you heard for the appearance of the rainbow?

One fine morning long ago, a hunter shot a duck with a newly made arrow. The arrow did not harm the duck, but settled deep in her feathers. When she flew away, the arrow flew with her.

To the hunter, this was a very special arrow, so he followed the duck, hoping to get it back. All day he pursued the duck until he was completely lost, but still he went on. He followed the duck to the far side of the ocean. When finally he reached the opposite shore, there was a surprise waiting. The duck had changed into a giant woman!

"Now I have you!" screamed the giant as she snatched the hunter. "I've been waiting to catch a new husband, and here you are!" Grabbing a hank of the hunter's hair, the giantess pulled him along beside her. On their way to her house, they passed a neighbor, who whispered a few words of caution to the hunter.

"Watch out! Tonight she'll kill you and eat you, just like the others!"

Late that night when the hunter thought the giant was asleep, he escaped. He dashed through the trees, over the hills and along the water until once more he was lost. He could hear the giant woman's thundering footsteps in the distance. Suddenly a beautiful woman dressed in cloth of many colors appeared in his path.

Stopping to catch his breath, the hunter asked, "Who are you?"

"I am Rainbow Woman," said the stranger. "Why are you running so fast?"

"Don't you feel the earth tremble?" said the hunter. "Those are the footsteps of an evil giant who wants to kill me."

"Then I can help you," replied Rainbow Woman. "Run on ahead. I'll follow in a moment."

Woman

Many folk tales offer explanations for mysterious natural occurrences, such as the change of seasons, the weather, and unusual plants and animals. This traditional oral tale from the Hoh and Quileute tribes explains the origin of the rainbow. It was written down at the turn of the century.

When Rainbow Woman caught up with the hunter, they could hear the giant woman thumping down the path, shaking all the trees as she rumbled along. Then, WOOMP! and everything was silent.

"What did you do?" asked the hunter.

"I set a trap," said Rainbow Woman. "Now, come along and rest at my house," she said, for already she loved him.

So the hunter went off with the beautiful Rainbow Woman and by morning he had fallen in love too.

The hunter married Rainbow Woman and after a while, they had a child. But one morning the hunter took his bow and arrows, as he often did, and went hunting. When he had not returned by afternoon, Rainbow Woman went out to look for him, but she could not find him. To this day, he has not returned.

Rainbow Woman knows her husband has just lost his way again, so she keeps watch faithfully. Sometimes she climbs into the sky so she can see better to search the land. When we see a double rainbow, we know her child is searching with her, too.

Author GRETCHEN WILL MAYO *has degrees in journalism and teaching. She is also a painter and occasionally illustrates her own books.*

EXPRESS
YOURSELF

Think of a natural phenomenon and the kind of tale you would create to explain its origin. Would you use a humorous approach, or would you be more straightforward? Why?

Adapted from Good Grief!
The Story of Charles M. Schulz
by Rheta Grimsley Johnson

Working for
PEANUTS

What does it take for a comic strip to develop a loyal following?

"Where do you get your ideas?" is by far the most commonly asked question of any cartoonist, and for most it is a continual source of consternation. It's like asking a carpenter, "Where did you get that house?" He can either respond with the obvious "I built it" or with the intricate "Well, I went down to the hardware store and got some nails and wood. . . ." Both replies would be equally accurate and unenlightening. But no one would ask a carpenter that, because people can see where the house came from.

In truth, what goes into a good house goes into a good cartoon: skill, thought, and hard work. Yet because it all occurs between the cartoonist's ears, it seems more like magic. The good cartoonist looks at the same thing as everybody else and then produces a drawing of something nobody else saw. The good cartoonist works so hard to kindle his innate spark that he is amazed when reminded his doodles don't necessarily reflect all that hard work. Of course, bad cartoonists simply think that they're geniuses.

A more precise question would be, "How do you do it?" Equally difficult to answer, perhaps, but at least the cartoonist might reply, "It's my gift, and I've worked hard to develop it."

For forty years Charles Schulz has worked hard, and he has his routine about nailed down. He doesn't worry, as his father did in the early days, that he won't continue to come up with a new gag every day. If he has a professional anxiety, it is that his originality will fail him, that he will never come up with another innovative device that will catch the readers' imaginations and set *Peanuts* apart from the pack.

Schulz identifies twelve such devices that have worked so well he is willing to attribute to them his strip's historic popularity. He is particularly proud of these ideas, for they are products of his unique intellect, things no one else would have thought of. Or at least no one did. To Schulz, the twelve things that helped make *Peanuts* are:

The Kite-Eating Tree

"One of the first things that really worked for me was Charlie Brown getting that dumb kite caught in the tree," says Schulz. "He was standing there all week long, looking at it. And people loved it." The introduction of the kite-eating tree was one of the first *Peanuts* stories to continue throughout a whole week, as one by one Charlie Brown's friends came by to comment on his problem.

The Baseball Games

The point of the baseball gimmick is the losing, of course. Besides Snoopy, probably nothing has come to typify *Peanuts* more than Charlie Brown going down in flames on his pitcher's mound one more time. On the rare occasion when victory is near, Charlie Brown manages to lose the day. Charlie

Cartoonist Charles Schulz points to twelve ideas that worked for him.

Brown wants to win so badly. He tries so hard. It's something every reader who happens to be human can understand.

Linus's Blanket

The blanket has provided another way for Schulz to let his drawings tell stories in a way words could never do. Linus wields it like a whip, folds it into unlikely shapes, and wages wars with Snoopy over it. The blanket has been cut up, ripped, stomped on, tailored into sports coats, and nearly burned up.

Lucy's Psychiatry Booth

What did Charles Schulz mean when he put Lucy behind that booth? Only one thing is certain. He thought it would be funny. "The booth really was a takeoff on the lemonade stands that appeared for years in other kid strips," explains Schulz.

PEANUTS REPRINTED BY PERMISSION OF UFS INC.

Schroeder's Music

Schroeder quickly established himself as a musician, playing the toy piano before he could talk. His music has provided numerous opportunities for visual jokes: other characters bump into the notes, birds sit on them, and Charlie Brown's kite even gets tangled in them. "The piano idea actually came from a small toy piano we had bought for our three-year-old daughter Meredith," says Schulz.

Snoopy's Doghouse

In the beginning, Snoopy actually slept in his doghouse with his head drooping out the door—just like a real dog. But Snoopy is more than a real dog. Now he sleeps on top of his house, and readers never get to see inside. Their curiosity is only teased as he pulls out album collections, a pool table, or paintings by famous artists.

Snoopy Himself

Face it, Charlie Brown, Snoopy has stolen the show. Snoopy helped bring your neighborhood out of the ordinary and into a unique world where dogs compose stories on typewriters and invite birds over to play dominoes.

The Red Baron

When Schulz introduced Snoopy the World War I Flying Ace in 1965, *Peanuts* reached even higher pinnacles of popularity. Schulz's son Monte takes credit for giving his dad the idea for the Red Baron sequences, since he had been collecting models of World War I aircraft at the time the strips began.

Woodstock

To be a totally effective comedian, Snoopy needed a side-kick, so along came the small and yellow Woodstock. Woodstock (named after the famous concert in a rural New York town) was simply a formalized version of Snoopy's feathered followers who had been hovering around the doghouse for years.

The Football Episodes

Besides the constant losing, the running-and-falling gag—when Lucy pulls the football away from Charlie Brown—is an example of another element that Schulz uses so well: repetition. Once a newspaper editor cancelled *Peanuts*, complaining that the author did the same things over and over. He was quickly forced to reinstate the comic strip, with an apology, when his disappointed readers set up a postal howl.

The Great Pumpkin

Linus is the most intellectual of the *Peanuts* characters, but he also is the most innocent. Despite his yearly dose of reality, he never forsakes his mistaken notion that something called the Great Pumpkin is going to bring him gifts.

The Little Red-Haired Girl

The little red-haired girl has never been shown in the *Peanuts* strip (Schulz does not count the animated version), and he believes she never will be. She is best worshipped from afar. Love remains at a distance. The football is never kicked. The Great Pumpkin never comes. The winning run is never scored.

RHETA GRIMSLEY JOHNSON *writes a syndicated newspaper column and has received several journalism awards. Her husband is cartoonist Jimmy Johnson, creator of the "Arlo and Janis" comic strip.*

EXPRESS YOURSELF

Which of Schulz's twelve devices is your favourite? Why?

The last car drove away. It began to rain.

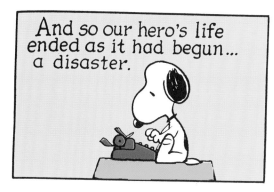
And *so* our hero's life ended as it had begun... a disaster.

"I never got any breaks," he had always complained.

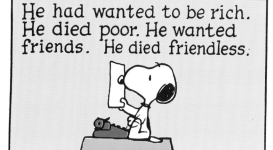
He had wanted to be rich. He died poor. He wanted friends. He died friendless.

He wanted to be loved. He died unloved. He wanted laughter. He found only tears.

He wanted applause. He received boos. He wanted fame. He found only obscurity. He wanted answers. He found only questions.

I'M HAVING A HARD TIME ENDING THIS..

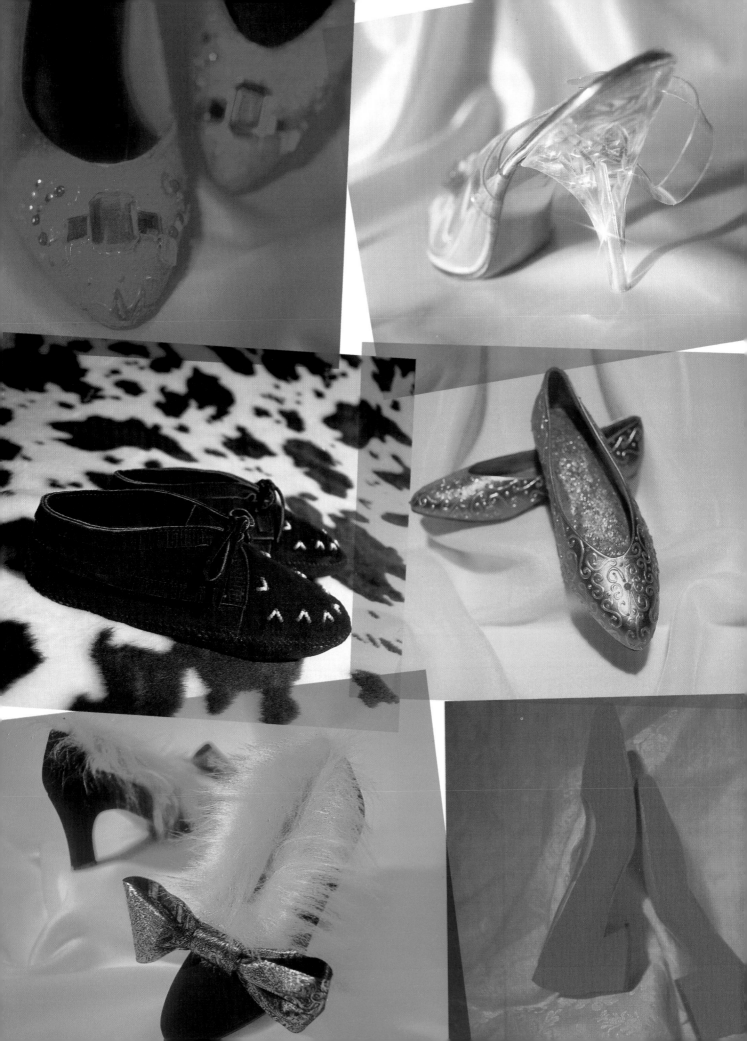

900 Cinderellas

By Judith C. Greenfield

What is it about this story that appeals to so many people?

NO MATTER WHERE YOU GO IN THE WORLD, IT'S LIKELY CINDERELLA GOT THERE FIRST!

If a poll were taken to determine the best-loved fairy tale in the world, the result would probably be "Cinderella." The Chinese call Cinderella Yeh-Shen. In Vietnam, she is called Cam. Her German name is Aschenputtel. Algonquin Indians know her as Little Burnt Face.

No matter what she is called, she is a virtuous and beautiful young woman. Members of her family are cruel to her, often out of jealousy. She is forced to wear ragged clothes and do lowly work. A magical person or thing comes to her aid. Disguised in beautiful clothes, Cinderella meets a handsome man, often a king or a prince, who wants to marry her. She flees or hides from him, but eventually he finds her. Back in her tattered clothes, she proves her identity in some special test. The young woman and man marry and live happily ever after. There are at least 900 different versions of the story in Europe and Asia, but basically they all follow this plot. . . .

The Vietnamese story "The Jeweled Slipper" involves a magic fish and bones. This story also emphasizes an intense rivalry, this time between two sisters. Tam is jealous of her lovely sister Cam. She kills Cam's [pet] fish, but a genie turns the bones into jeweled slippers. A black crow drops one slipper in the king's garden. . . . The king falls in love with the slipper and determines to marry its owner. He finds Cam and proposes marriage. But wicked Tam hits Cam on the head just before the marriage takes place. Cam suffers amnesia and disappears. When the king finds her, he produces the slipper, and suddenly Cam remembers everything. She marries the king and lures Tam into a caldron of boiling water.

A Frenchman named Charles Perrault wrote the most familiar Western version of "Cinderella." Perrault lived during the 17th century, when fairy tales were very popular at the elegant court of King Louis XIV. Perrault spent time at the king's court, knew the stories circulating there, and rewrote them to entertain his own children at home.

His story "Cendrillon" introduced a fairy godmother as the magical helper. She turns Cinderella's rags into exquisite clothes and changes a pumpkin into a golden coach. Most important of all, she provides dancing slippers made of glass. People have debated as to whether Perrault meant the slipper to be glass (*verre* in French) or fur (*vair*). But no matter what he intended, he is responsible for the famous glass slipper as an identity test. Also, although covered by cinders and dirt, Perrault's Cinderella can fit into the slipper because of the goodness in her heart. Perrault teaches the moral that people should be judged by their inner beauty, not by fancy clothes or outward appearances.

More than a century later, the brothers Jakob and Wilhelm Grimm collected many folktales and fairy tales from all over Germany. Their Cinderella is called Aschenputtel, and she, too, has a cruel stepmother and stepsisters. She receives her dazzling ball gown and golden slippers from a magical white bird perched on a hazel tree growing over her mother's grave. She loses a slipper while fleeing from the ball, and the prince finds it and searches for its owner. One stepsister cuts off her toes and another her heel to try to squeeze into the tiny shoe. Their bleeding feet identify them as "false brides." On Aschenputtel's wedding day, birds peck out the stepsisters' eyes.

What happened to this story when people from Europe settled years ago in the Appalachian Mountains of North Carolina? They changed some details to fit their language and new surroundings. Their heroine, Ashpet, longs to go not to a ball but to a church meeting. Jealous of her beauty, the women who hire her hide her under a washtub. Her fairy godmother, an old witch woman living in the mountains, provides a "pretty red dress" and "the prettiest red slippers—the littlest 'uns you ever saw." Prince Charming is still the king's son, although here he is known as "the king's boy." These details show that this is a Cinderella story transplanted to American soil.

European settlers told "Cinderella" to Algonquin tribes, such as the Micmacs, who changed it to fit their culture. In their version of the story, two older daughters of a great chief scar their young, gentle sister with hot ashes. But through her honesty, Little Burnt Face proves that she is worthy to marry a god named the Invisible One. Only she can see his bowstring made of a rainbow and his shoulder strap made of the Milky Way.

How and why did the Cinderella story appear all over the world? Some scholars say that the entire story started in just one place and was carried by word of mouth to other countries, where it was changed to fit local customs. Others believe that the story arose independently in different societies because it expresses universal fears and hopes. They say that people everywhere created their own Cinderella stories and that only *some* of the details, like the tiny slipper, spread from country to country. All agree that the story has something for everyone—magic, romance, elevation in social status, unfairness punished, and goodness rewarded.

JUDITH C. GREENFIELD *is a children's librarian in New York and has taught storytelling to both children and adults.*

Cinderella Plays Football

Yes, and not only that, but she also runs for political office . . . and wins!

Sports teams having a surprisingly successful season are often called "Cinderella teams." For example, if a team finishes in last place one year and then goes to the playoffs the next year, headlines are likely to proclaim: Cinderella Season Surprises Experts!

Rags-to-riches references to Cinderella are also popular in politics. An unknown candidate who manages to get elected is said to have run a "Cinderella campaign."

By Roland H. Sherwood

Why do people love to exaggerate when they tell stories?

The tall tale, the humorous fable, and the unbelievable yarn are told from one end of the country to the other, and like a rolling snowball, gain with each roll-around, for the popularity of the tall tale can never be doubted. Once told, it is repeated time and time again.

The art of tall story telling is to make the yarn sound logical: that is, until the last line—and to do it with a straight face.

The weather is always good for a tall tale or two. A fellow in Campbellton, New Brunswick, said it got so cold up there that when a person spoke the words immediately froze and nothing could be heard. "If you wanted to know what was said," the Campbellton man said, "you had to take the words inside and thaw them out."

That same winter, the storytellers say, hunters didn't use snares or shells to get rabbits. They just set out lighted lanterns along the rabbit runs. When a rabbit stopped to warm his paws at the light, the hunter rapped it over the head and carried it home.

As is customary with tall story tellers, each tries to 'out-yarn' the others. One such storyteller said he remembered that bitter winter very well. He was one who set out the lanterns for the rabbits. One day it was so cold that the lantern flame was very dim. "On investigation," he said, "I found the lantern flame had frozen. I pinched the

Tales *of* Winter

flame off and threw it away. Know what happened? When spring came the flame thawed out and set fire to a nearby cabin."

A fellow from Pictou said that while out game hunting he used up all his ammunition with the exception of one bullet. "On my way home," he said, "I came face to face with two bears, and both were ugly. They took after me and I took off on the fly. I was tiring fast and the bears were gaining on me. I knew I had to do something pretty fast, so I whipped out my hunting knife, stuck it in a stump with the blade facing me. When the bears came raging along the trail, I took aim at the knife blade and fired. My bullet hit the knife blade, split in two and each half killed a bear. The recoil of the rifle knocked me into the nearby stream and I came up with a pocketful of fish."

ROLAND H. SHERWOOD *has worked as a play-wright, actor, writer, and TV producer. During his twelve-year radio career he was called "The Master Storyteller of the Maritimes."*

EXPRESS

YOURSELF

Under what circumstances do you hear or tell stories that rely on exaggeration for their effect? Write a tall tale you or a friend would be likely to tell.

Imagine that you could hire a team of famous writers to help you work on your next writing assignment.

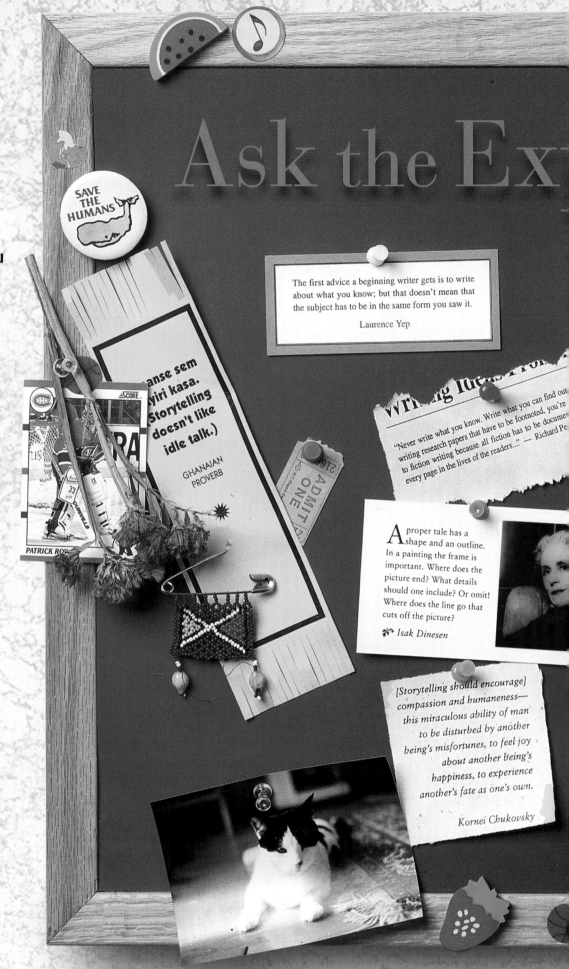

The first advice a beginning writer gets is to write about what you know; but that doesn't mean that the subject has to be in the same form you saw it.

Laurence Yep

anse sem yiri kasa. (Storytelling doesn't like idle talk.)

GHANAIAN PROVERB

Writing Ideas From

"Never write what you know. Write what you can find out... writing research papers that have to be footnoted, you're to fiction writing because all fiction has to be documen every page in the lives of the readers..." — Richard Pe

A proper tale has a shape and an outline. In a painting the frame is important. Where does the picture end? What details should one include? Or omit! Where does the line go that cuts off the picture?

🌾 Isak Dinesen

[Storytelling should encourage] compassion and humaneness— this miraculous ability of man to be disturbed by another being's misfortunes, to feel joy about another being's happiness, to experience another's fate as one's own.

Kornei Chukovsky

erts

"Reading, though, is the way to learn to write. Someone interested in writing should just read, without looking at all the structures and strategy of the writing. Writers can show you directions. We're all influenced by the people we read to one degree or another, and we shouldn't deny those influences. Other people show us what is possible."
— Carol Shields, author, interviewed by Andrew Garrod in *Speaking for Myself: Canadian Writers in Interview* (1986).

If a writer stops observing he is finished. But he does not have to observe consciously nor think how it will be useful.
— Ernest Hemingway

Write freely and as rapidly as possible and throw the whole thing on paper. Never correct or rewrite until the whole thing is down. Rewrite in process is usually found to be an excuse for not going on. It also interferes with flow and rhythm which can only come from a kind of unconscious association with the material.

John Steinbeck

Once you're into a story everything seems to apply—what you overhear on a city bus is exactly what your character would say on the page you're writing. Wherever you go, you meet part of your story. I guess you're tuned in for it, and the right things are sort of magnetized—if you can think of your ears as magnets.

EUDORA WELTY

The first drafts are always the most difficult. They're a lot of hard work. Second and third drafts are easier. That's where you can really let yourself go.... Knowing when to stop is an important instinct.

— Pierre Berton

The wastepaper basket is the writer's best friend.   — Isaac Bashevis Singer

Jody
2:30

Fall seven times, stand up eight.
— Japanese Proverb

FIRST PLACE

SHARE EARTH

Joe SAKIC
SCORE '92   NORDIQUES

By Barbara Greenwood

FEASTING *with Words*

What does it take to be a master storyteller?

Tololwa M. Mollel burst onto the children's publishing scene in 1990 with a haunting tale about *The Orphan Boy*, adopted and loved by an old man until curiosity overcame the old man's common sense. Text and pictures together transformed a Maasai creation myth into a poignant tale of loneliness touched by celestial mystery.

IN THE AFRICAN MAASAI LANGUAGE, A CONVERSATION IS CALLED "FEASTING WITH WORDS." STORIES PROVIDE A REAL BANQUET!

His second book, *Rhinos for Lunch and Elephants for Supper,* is a comic/scary tale about a hare who returns to her cave one day to hear a small noise. "Who's there?" she calls and a voice booms back "A monster. A MONSTER! I eat rhinos for lunch and elephants for supper. Come in if you dare." This challenge triggers off a series of comic confrontations as larger and larger animals try to out-shout the monster.

Who is the man behind these tales? He is a doctoral student from the University of Alberta, an actor and lecturer in drama both in Edmonton and in his native Tanzania, the author of short stories aired on the B.B.C. and a storyteller in three languages: Swahili, a Maasai dialect and English.

The voice is the voice of a storyteller— warm, flexible, capable of purring softly or roaring like a lion, inflecting to suggest the absurdity of a situation, softening to underline gravity, or, for the comic/scary *Rhinos,* rollercoastering up and down the scale.

Tololwa got his start at storytelling on his grandfather's coffee farm in Tanzania. "He was a workaholic so the only saving grace when you went to the farm was that he told a lot of stories. That made the work a little more enjoyable. So he would tell stories about the Second World War when he was growing up and about aspects of Maasai

ILLUSTRATION BY PAUL MORIN

culture that I did not know because I didn't grow up speaking Maasai."

Listening was fascinating but Tololwa's grandfather then turned the tables and demanded stories in return. "He always expected me to tell him about current affairs. He had only been up to Grade 2 but he had a real hunger for knowledge. That was the time of the Vietnam war so I had to find a way of explaining to him about anti-ballistic missiles. There was no vocabulary for this in Maasai so I had to use a lot of gestures. I'd see him nodding his head, following every word. Then he'd say, 'Can you repeat that?' I really had to be up on things because he could be really hot-tempered. . . .

"Growing up I listened to stories from grandmother but it wasn't until I started reading to my first son that I said to myself, 'Ah, this is nice. The idea that someone can write a story for children and it would also appeal to me. I'd like to write like this.' And the simplicity of the traditional tale! The one where the hen said, 'who is going to grow the wheat' and all the animals say, 'Not I! Not I!' The idea that someone can take something so simple and use it to say something important really appealed to me. So I said to myself, I guess there are a lot of traditional African tales that would work this way, could become a vehicle for some large idea, some large concept."

BARBARA GREENWOOD *is a Toronto-based writer and teacher who is now working on a book about pioneers.*

EXPRESS
YOUR SELF

When do you and your friends or family exchange stories? What kinds of stories are they?

To prepare his award-winning illustrations for Mollel's *The Orphan Boy*, artist Paul Morin spent two months in Africa sketching scenery and characters.

STO

WITH

WO

Peruvian craftspeople carve stories or scenes on dried gourds (fruits similar to squash). The tiny drawings on this gourd show armadillos, crocodiles, and people knitting and carving.

RIES

UT

RDS

How many times have you seen or heard a story without even realizing it?

You stare at a gripping photograph in the newspaper. Without reading the accompanying article, you can tell what it's going to say. The photograph told the story.

You turn on the television one Saturday morning and find cartoons. If you close your eyes, the music probably keeps you informed about what's going on.

All around you stories are being told, and if you look for them only in the form of words strung together, you'll miss out. Look for stories everywhere, and you'll find them coming from cultures whose languages you don't understand, from video games you play, and who knows where else!

y Balinese dances based on the *nabharata* and the *nayana*, the two atest epic poems g heroic stories) of a. These ancient ns describe the entures of Hindu lty. Balinese cers use hand gestures to help "tell" s of these stories.

The Bayeux tapestry is a 70-metre-long story about William the Conqueror's eleventh-century invasion of England. The section pictured above shows how Harold I, a king of England, was told about Halley's Comet.

SCORE 7500
TIME 0:25
RINGS 14

SONIC × 4

In video games such as the one pictured here, a player's skill determines the outcome of the plot and the fate of the animated characters.

DRAWING BY CHAS. ADDAMS; © 1940, 1968 THE NEW YORKER MAGAZINE, INC.

Cartoons often tell humorous stories that wouldn't be funny in words.

Mimes enact miniature stories through facial expressions and body movements. Here, a mime struggles to open a stuck door. When he is convinced it will not open, he leans against it for support, and then it gives way.

WITHOUT

This Aboriginal bark painting from Australia tells the story of a funeral and shows the pathway of the spirit after death.

WORDS

EDITING
History

What if telling the truth were illegal?

Did you ever have *one of those days*—a day you'd like to erase from your memory and edit out of the memory of anyone who witnessed it? If you ever wrote the story of your life, you'd be sure to leave that day out!

Writers of autobiographies and memoirs erase days, episodes, and characters from their lives all the time. To be fair, they can't include everything. Some details must be edited out, others played down, and still others highlighted in order for the story to hold together and make sense. Everyone goes through a similar sorting process when describing an event. You do it when you tell your sister what happened in science class: you leave out the part about sharpening your pencil because your focus is the explosion of the teacher's experiment. If you were to turn the incident into a fictional short story, you might not only leave out

particular elements but also change others in order to heighten the effect.

Historians, who try to tell the "true" story of the past, must also decide what to include, what to emphasize, and what to play down. Otherwise, telling the history of the Hundred Years War would take longer than the war itself! What's more, it wouldn't add much to our understanding of the events.

Photographs don't always tell the truth. The outline next to Klement Gottwald indicates how a figure might be "airbrushed out." An airbrush sprays a fine mist of ink or paint. To "airbrush out" an image from a photograph, the artist covers the image with the same colours that appear behind it.

The adjective **solicitous** means "concerned or troubled," and comes from the Latin word *sollicitare*, meaning "to disturb, agitate, or entreat." Today solicitors, or lawyers, are paid to prepare cases on behalf of those they are representing.

But who has the right to decide what to leave out? Can anyone weigh these decisions fairly, without being influenced by current politics, or by personal opinions about who or what is right or wrong?

One solution is to open history-telling to as many different people as possible. That way, the story is likely to be told from many points of view, based upon a variety of sources. Then readers and listeners can compare accounts and decide which ones are trustworthy.

But what happens when writing different versions of history is illegal? What if a government decides which versions can be told and punishes anyone who writes a different account? In some countries, that's exactly what happens—it's called censorship.

Vladimír Clementis, born in Czechoslovakia in 1902, was a journalist, critic, and politician. For a while he enjoyed the status of being part of the Communist government's "in" crowd. However, he quickly found himself on the outside when he started writing material that was considered unacceptable by the government.

Then the Czech government took an extreme step. It tried to erase Clementis from history.

Milan Kundera, another Czechoslovakian writer, described the Clementis incident, in his book, *The Book of Laughter and Forgetting*: "In Feburary 1948, Communist leader Klement Gottwald stepped out on the balcony of a Baroque palace in Prague to address the hundreds of thousands of his fellow citizens packed into Old Town Square. It was a crucial moment in Czech history—a fateful moment of the kind that occurs once or twice in a millennium.

"Gottwald was flanked by his comrades, with Clementis standing next to him. There were snow flurries, it was cold, and Gottwald was bareheaded. The solicitous Clementis took off his own fur cap and set it on Gottwald's head.

"The Party propaganda section put out hundreds of thousands of copies of a photograph of that balcony with Gottwald, a fur cap on his head and comrades at his side, speaking to the nation. On that balcony the history of Communist Czechoslovakia was born. Every child knew the photograph from posters, schoolbooks, and museums.

"Four years later Clementis was charged with treason and hanged. The propaganda section immediately airbrushed him out of history and, obviously, out of all the photographs as well. Ever since, Gottwald has stood on that balcony alone. Where Clementis once stood, there is only bare palace wall. All that remains of Clementis is the cap on Gottwald's head."

Because of his anti-government writings, Kundera lost his job and his books were banned. When he published *The Book of Laughter and Forgetting*, his citizenship was taken away as well.

When was the last time you heard or read a true story and knew that you were getting only part of the picture? Why do you think the story was told that way?

The Many Lives of
ROMEO
and
JULIET

No matter how many times people encounter this tragic tale, they still love it.

When retelling a story, how much can you change without losing the power of the original?

How do you recognize a really good story? One way to measure a story's success is to ask the following questions: First, how long has it been around? Has the story survived through several generations, even through many centuries? Second, does the story attract a wide audience—people in different countries, professions, and age groups? Third, does the story appeal to something basic or deep in human nature? Do people enjoy it over and over again? Do creative artists constantly rework the story, changing details yet keeping its basic core? If you can answer yes to these questions, you've found a classic—like the story of Romeo and Juliet.

The most familiar version of Romeo and Juliet is the play by William Shakespeare. Set in fourteenth-century Verona, Italy, it focusses on the fate of two teenagers who are desperately in love. Their families, the Montagues and the Capulets, are bitter enemies, involved in a feud that often leads to bloodshed. When Juliet's family hosts a ball, Romeo Montague crashes it in disguise. Romeo and Juliet dance and fall in love. After the ball, during a now-famous balcony scene, Romeo and Juliet declare their love in spite of the difficulties they know lie ahead. Later, they enlist

A nineteenth-century engraving of Romeo and Juliet

the aid of a kindly clergyman, Friar Lawrence, and are secretly married.

Soon after, Romeo's friend Mercutio is killed in a street fight by Juliet's cousin Tybalt. Enraged by his friend's death, Romeo kills Tybalt. As punishment, Romeo is forced to leave Verona. Meanwhile, Juliet's father intends to force her to marry another man. To escape this marriage, Juliet devises a trick. She takes a sleeping potion that will make her look as though she has died. Romeo returns and finds Juliet apparently dead. Grief-stricken, he drinks poison. A few moments later, Juliet awakens and finds Romeo dead. Determined to join him, she stabs herself and dies. The Capulet and Montague families grieve the loss of these young people and in their grief discover a common bond. The fighting between the two families ends.

At the heart of the story's appeal, of course, are the "star-crossed lovers," Romeo and Juliet, who struggle to hold onto love in a hostile world. They are so devoted that they are unwilling to live without each other. Nothing can prevent their true love, but hatred can and does cost the teenagers their lives. In the end, love's only triumph is in bringing the grieving families together.

Anyone who has experienced the joys and sorrows of being in love, or who has struggled with the consequences of loving the

◀ Dancers Rex Harrington and Karen Kain of the National Ballet of Canada portray Romeo and Juliet.

"wrong" person, can identify with Romeo and Juliet. The story touches deep feelings in audiences of all ages. That's one reason creative artists—composers, choreographers, dancers, filmmakers, dramatists, writers, and painters—have repeatedly retold the story, each giving it a unique slant.

A high school performance of *Romeo and Juliet*

Even Shakespeare, whose magnificent poetry enhanced the tale, borrowed the story. His 1595 play is most likely based on Edward Brooke's 1562 poem "The Tragical History of Romeo and Juliet." Brooke's poem, in turn, is strikingly similar to earlier Italian tales. A nineteenth-century opera by Charles Gounod provides a good demonstration of how and why a recognized masterpiece like Shakespeare's might undergo changes. In this version, Romeo's death is slightly postponed—in order to allow the lovers to sing a last romantic duet before their deaths!

Almost one hundred years later, two Russian writers, Sergei Radlov and Adrian Piatrovsky, wanted to retell the story in ballet form. They, too, planned to change Shakespeare's ending—this time to a happy

WORD TALK

The term **star-crossed lovers** was coined by Shakespeare in his play *Romeo and Juliet*. To be star-crossed means "to be doomed to unhappiness by an unlucky arrangement of the stars and planets." Astrology, the study of the heavens and belief in their influence on human affairs, was practised in many ancient civilizations and is still popular today.

one in which Friar Lawrence prevents Romeo from stabbing himself. When the Russian composer Sergei Prokofiev began working on the music, however, he realized that the meaning and impact of the story depended on the death of the two lovers. Prokofiev's *Romeo and Juliet,* a ballet in three acts, was first produced in Leningrad in 1940 and remained true to Shakespeare's ending. Retelling the story using only music and movement meant eliminating episodes of Shakespeare's play that could not easily be told without words. But, as anyone who has seen the ballet knows, music and dance also added to the story, expressing a sadness and joy that words alone could not.

Not long after the debut of Prokofiev's ballet, yet another version of the story appeared, this one combining music and dance with words. In the 1950s four remarkable artists—choreographer Jerome Robbins, writer Arthur Laurents, lyricist Stephen Sondheim, and composer Leonard Bernstein—began work on a modern interpretation of Shakespeare's *Romeo and Juliet*. The result was the Broadway musical *West Side Story*. The idea began with Jerome Robbins. In the late 1940s, as he helped a young actor rehearse the part of Shakespeare's Romeo, Robbins wondered what Romeo would be like if he lived

ANYONE WHO HAS EXPERIENCED THE JOYS AND SORROWS OF BEING IN LOVE... CAN IDENTIFY WITH ROMEO AND JULIET.

today. From this simple question, the idea of doing a modern, musical version of Shakespeare's *Romeo and Juliet,* set in New York City instead of Verona, was born. Composer Leonard Bernstein described his excitement with the project and its modern portrayal of the warring families: "We're fired again by the Romeo notion . . . and have come up with what I think is going to be it: two teenage gangs."

Although *West Side Story* retains the essence of the original plot and many of Shake-

Maria (Natalie Wood) and Tony (Richard Beymer) profess their love in the 1961 film *West Side Story.*

speare's characters, there are also many changes. For example, Shakespeare's lovers meet at a ball, whereas *West Side Story*'s Maria and Tony meet at a high-school dance. The warring families of Shakespeare's story are replaced by warring gangs. Romeo and Juliet declare their love on a balcony, Maria and Tony on a fire escape. Friar Lawrence helps Shakespeare's hero and heroine; Doc, the local pharmacist, assists Maria and Tony. Again, the most important change is in the ending. Though the musical does not end happily, both lovers do not die in *West Side Story*: Tony is killed but Maria lives.

The enduring story of Romeo and Juliet expresses both our hope that love indeed will conquer all and our fear that something evil will tear love apart. It is a story that will never grow old. Perhaps, even now, a group of people somewhere is working out ideas for a new and up-to-the-minute Romeo and Juliet.

EXPRESS
YOURSELF

If you were to create a contemporary version of *Romeo and Juliet,* where would you set the story of the star-crossed lovers? How would they meet each other? What forces would threaten their love? Would they live or die?

THE BLACK-FLY SONG

BY WADE HEMSWORTH

Singer and songwriter Wade Hemsworth worked for a time as a draftsperson for Ontario Hydro. In the fall of 1949, he travelled with a survey crew to the Little Abitibi River, where Ontario Hydro was planning to build a dam. Hemsworth wrote this song about the experience.

'Twas early in the spring when I decide to go For to work up in the woods in North Ontario, And the unemployment office said they'd send me through To the Little Abitibi with the survey crew.

REFRAIN

And the black-flies the little black-flies, Always the black-fly no matter where you go, I'll die with the black-fly a-pickin' my bones In North Ontario, i-o, in North Ontario.

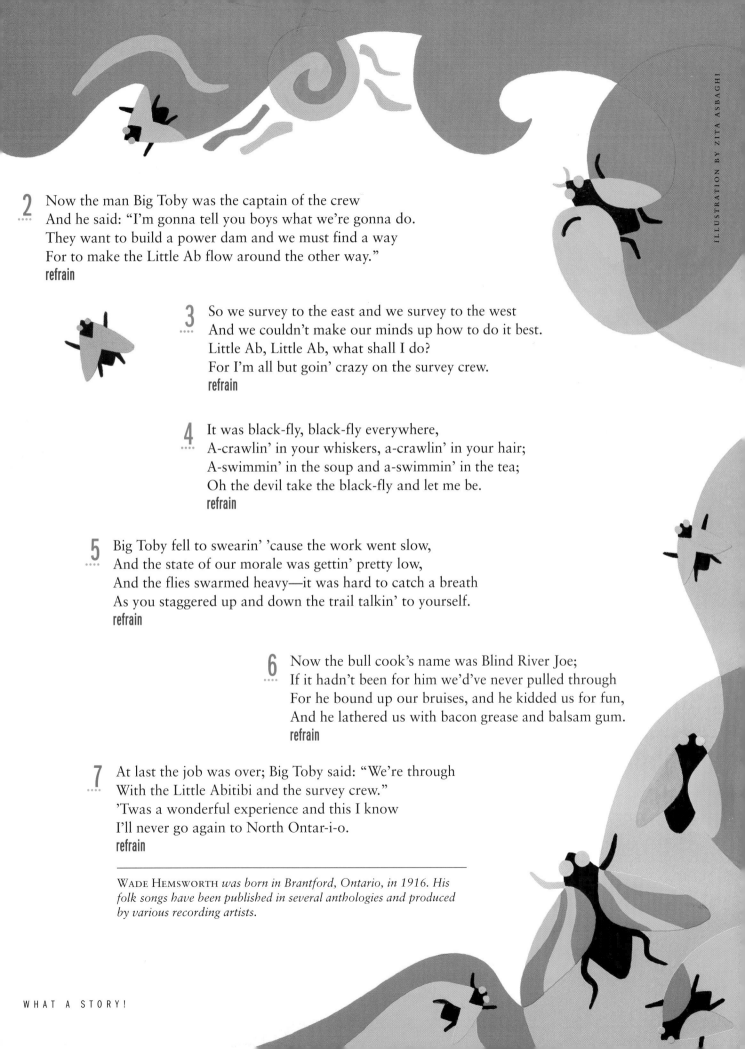

ILLUSTRATION BY ZITA ASBAGHI

2 Now the man Big Toby was the captain of the crew
And he said: "I'm gonna tell you boys what we're gonna do.
They want to build a power dam and we must find a way
For to make the Little Ab flow around the other way."
refrain

3 So we survey to the east and we survey to the west
And we couldn't make our minds up how to do it best.
Little Ab, Little Ab, what shall I do?
For I'm all but goin' crazy on the survey crew.
refrain

4 It was black-fly, black-fly everywhere,
A-crawlin' in your whiskers, a-crawlin' in your hair;
A-swimmin' in the soup and a-swimmin' in the tea;
Oh the devil take the black-fly and let me be.
refrain

5 Big Toby fell to swearin' 'cause the work went slow,
And the state of our morale was gettin' pretty low,
And the flies swarmed heavy—it was hard to catch a breath
As you staggered up and down the trail talkin' to yourself.
refrain

6 Now the bull cook's name was Blind River Joe;
If it hadn't been for him we'd've never pulled through
For he bound up our bruises, and he kidded us for fun,
And he lathered us with bacon grease and balsam gum.
refrain

7 At last the job was over; Big Toby said: "We're through
With the Little Abitibi and the survey crew."
'Twas a wonderful experience and this I know
I'll never go again to North Ontar-i-o.
refrain

WADE HEMSWORTH *was born in Brantford, Ontario, in 1916. His folk songs have been published in several anthologies and produced by various recording artists.*

In touch with TRA

An Inuit sculptor and a Cree painter
are inspired by the
traditional stories of their peoples.

What kinds of stories inspire you?

STONES THAT BREATHE
BY LAURA EGGERTSON

With a hammer, a chisel and a big block of stone, David Ruben Piqtoukun brings images of the Arctic to southern Canada's doorstep. Attacking a stone slab is one way Piqtoukun copes with living in Toronto, about 6500 kilometres southeast of Paulatuk, his home-town on the northwest coast of the Northwest Territories.

"Most people look at a rock and it looks like a rock," the artist says. "Myself, when I look at a rock I see it has personality, character—there's something in the stone that's breathing.

"It's like one of those horror flicks, *The Rock That Breathes*," he jokes.

Piqtoukun's jade, soapstone, alabaster and marble sculptures range in size from a palm-sized bear to a three-tonne Inukshuk landmark. He is particularly fond of creating angry bears—he

identifies the bear as his animal spirit—when city tensions get to him.

"I've been collecting oral mythology from the old people in my hometown—stories that have never been documented," he says. "From a story you see all this imagery in your head and you can pick and choose."

The stories give him enough inspiration that he no longer fears sculptor's block—which occurred about eight years ago, when "a rock was starting to look like a rock again."

Although his original motivation for sculpting was earning a living, Piqtoukun says that changed when he listened to the old people.

"I realized I was learning about my background through listening to the stories, carving and creating all the imagery," he says.

LAURA EGGERTSON, *born in 1962 in Winnipeg, Manitoba, has been a newspaper reporter for the Canadian Press wire service since 1987.*

David Piqtoukun travels regularly to the Arctic for inspiration and materials.

40

DITION

Piqtoukun created this sculpture, called *Shaman,* in 1982 from black and green stone and ivory.

CHRONICLER OF THE CREE
BY MAX MACDONALD

"I do this because I cannot read or write—only my name. In the pictures I can tell the story of my people."

So powerfully told are the stories in those pictures that the artist who painted them and made this statement today has a publicly financed gallery bearing his name and devoted exclusively to his works and life.

That artist is Allen Sapp, a Cree Indian and former welfare recipient who was once eyed with suspicion for peddling his paintings on the streets of his home town, North Battleford, Saskatchewan. Now the city has honoured him by converting a one-time library into the Allen Sapp Gallery—The Gonor Collection.

Allen Sapp grew up on the Red Pheasant Reserve near North Battleford.

In earlier times, the Cree had hunted buffalo on the open plains in summer. In winter they retreated to the sheltered parklands of aspen, scrub willow and sloughs that divide the boreal forest of the north from the near treeless plains of the southwest. By the time of Sapp's birth, however, they had been forced onto reserves where they raised cattle, horses and chickens, and grew grain. These reserves are nestled in the western section of the Saskatchewan parkland region that

Leaving the Baby With the Lady, painted by Allen Sapp in 1970

swings in a gentle arc from halfway up the west side of the province to the far southeast corner.

Under Sapp's brush, the Cree people come alive as they go about the daily routines of family chores, cultural and spiritual gatherings, and simply earning a living. In his eyes, his people and the environment are one, linked through the spirit of nature (manito or manitou) to a reverence for all living things.

Allen Sapp today is a man whose identity crisis is long over and whose pride of heritage is apparent in the Indian dress he wears and the Indian customs he embraces. But mostly that pride is reflected in his paintings. There are no cars or power lines or plumbing fixtures in them. Instead, there are horses, kerosene lamps and lanterns, huge piles of firewood and barrels of water. There are powwows and rodeos and the solemnity of funerals. There are meals eaten squatting on the floor of sparsely furnished cabins, and others prepared over open fires outdoors in summer and winter. These

> "IN THE
> PICTURES
> I CAN
> TELL THE
> STORY OF
> MY PEOPLE."

and the log cabins, rail fences, grain harvesting, wood gathering, haying and searching for cattle all spell out a simple existence with gripping clarity. "Sapp's paintings," says [fellow artist] Wynona Mulcaster, "record the way it is, sometimes mean, sometimes sweet, but always with restraint, with freshness and complete honesty."

Indeed, in his winter scenes of horses and cattle humped against icy blasts with hoarfrost clinging to mouths and nostrils, there is a chill far more telling than the mere statement that the temperature once plunged to -57°C. In the same vein, verbal description says much less than Sapp's painting of youngsters intent on hockey games played on cleared sloughs.

And because these images flow so naturally from Sapp's memories of his Saskatchewan boyhood, they have touched many far removed from the artist and the source of his art.

MAX MACDONALD *was born in southeastern Saskatchewan in 1920. He has worked for newspapers in positions ranging from reporter to editor-in-chief.*

EXPRESS
YOURSELF

In what different ways might you illustrate a story that is meaningful to you? Choose one of your favourite stories and sketch or draft some ideas for portraying it visually.

THE
Sticks
OF *Truth*

Retold by George Shannon

What's not as easy as it first seems?
A riddle, of course. These puzzle stories have been popular for centuries. They are found worldwide in folk tales, children's rhymes, brainteasers, and classic mysteries solved by sleuths from Sherlock Holmes to Jessica Fletcher.

Are you as wise as this travelling judge?

ILLUSTRATION BY PAUL JERMANN

Long ago in India judges traveled from village to village. One day a judge stopped at an inn to rest, but the innkeeper was very upset. Someone had just that day stolen his daughter's gold ring. The judge told him not to worry and had all the guests gather so that he could question them. When he could not figure out from their answers who the thief was, the judge decided to use some old magic. He told them all he was going to have to use the sticks of truth.

"These are magic sticks," he explained, "that will catch the thief."

He gave each guest a stick to keep under their bed during the night.

"The stick belonging to the thief will grow two inches during the night. At breakfast we will all compare sticks and the longest stick will be the thief's."

The next morning the judge had all the guests come by his table and hold their sticks up next to his to see if they had grown. But one after another all were the same. None of them had grown any longer. Then suddenly the judge called, "This is the thief! Her stick is shorter than all the rest."

Once caught, the woman confessed and the ring was returned. But all the guests were confused about the sticks of truth. The judge had said the longest stick would be the thief's, but instead it had been the shortest stick.

Why?
(For the solution, turn to page 47.)

GEORGE SHANNON *tells stories to large audiences and writes tales for young people. This riddle comes from his collection* Stories to Solve.

EXPRESS
YOURSELF

What is the difference between a riddle and a joke? Which appeals to you more? Why? Ask your friends these questions and see if they agree with you.

Tales of a Trophy

If objects could talk, some would have surprising stories to tell. • *By Mac Davis*

The Stanley Cup, National Hockey League's most prized trophy, is awarded annually to the world-champion hockey team. It came into existence in 1893 when the Governor-General of Canada, Frederick Arthur, Lord Stanley of Preston, purchased it for less than forty-eight dollars. He then donated it as a special prize for the best hockey team extant. Winning the Stanley Cup is a professional team's outstanding achievement of the year. Strangely, this treasured trophy, which cost so little and survives as North America's oldest sports award, has had a curious history.

Over the years, several attempts were made to steal the famed Cup.

Once, a star player who had been given the honor of carrying the Stanley Cup to a victory banquet suddenly went berserk and kicked the silver trophy into the Rideau Canal in Ottawa. Fortunately, the canal was frozen over at the time, so the Stanley Cup wasn't lost forever. It was recovered slightly damaged.

Another time, the Cup was carelessly abandoned on a street corner by a player who had charge of it. It wasn't retrieved for many hours.

Still another time, an irate club owner thought so little of the

Calgary Flames celebrate winning the Stanley Cup.

Stanley Cup in his possession that he had to be restrained from throwing it into a lake.

Once, the players of a world-championship hockey team arrived with the Stanley Cup at a photographer's studio to pose for some special pictures. When that was done, they left the studio but forgot to take the Stanley Cup with them. It was months before the abandoned trophy was recovered from the studio basement.

Believe it or not, the coveted Stanley Cup was once left with an elderly lady who knew nothing of its prestigious value, and for a time, she used it as a flower pot. . . .

Once, a hockey team lost possession of the famed trophy when it was beaten in the Stanley Cup series, but the players refused to turn it over to the victors until they had had a riotous celebration of their own. So, winner and loser of the Stanley Cup engaged in a wild and fierce brawl for its possession.

Not too long ago, a thief broke into Hockey's Hall of Fame and stole the Stanley Cup. What he didn't know when he pulled off the robbery was that the Stanley Cup he filched was only a duplicate of the original. Some years ago a Danish silversmith created the replica which could be used for ceremonial purposes. That was the actual trophy taken by the invader.

Months later, the missing duplicate appeared as mysteriously as it had been stolen on the doorstep of a Toronto police constable.

Now the original Stanley Cup is safely ensconced in Hockey's Hall of Fame, as is its duplicate, waiting to be awarded to the world-champion team when the National Hockey League campaign reaches its climax with post-season play-offs each year.

MAC DAVIS, *born in 1905, has written many books about sports heroes and unusual sports happenings.*

The TV Commandments

An insider's view of television story writing • By J. Michael Straczynski

Here [is] the stuff nobody much talks about outside of the offices of story editors and producers—the absolutely essential elements in *any* telescript for *any* series.

• Maintain your focus on the star of the show, for whom, after all, your script is a vehicle. . . .

• Don't stretch your story too thin. . . . A good-sized act will consist of about five to seven *beats*. A beat is simply a unit of story action: *Jessica arrives at the airport, where she is picked up. Jessica arrives at the studio, where she is introduced to the people who have optioned her novel. A gate-crasher sneaks onto the studio and makes his way onto one of the sets.* Each of those three sentences is one beat. . . .

• But remember to move the camera around: Don't spend too much time in any one location. If you've spent four or five pages in the same set, reconsider your structure. . . .

• End each act on a dramatic high note—a complication that makes the viewer want to stick around after the commercial break. . . .

• Avoid convenience. Your characters must do things for a reason that makes sense to them,

not just because you want them to. . . .

• Try to make every scene do more than one thing at a time. You might, for instance, have all of your characters meet during a dinner scene. And that *might* be sufficient. But it's much better to take that scene and add a secret meeting between two of the characters in an adjoining room—a conference that another character overhears; and to have the dinner

conversation not just concern what's about to happen, but layer in the background of the characters, or establish their suspicions of one another. . . .

• Keep your guest characters different from one another. They must be distinct as individuals, no matter how similar they may be in class, social status or rank.

Give them different voices. Make them react in different ways to the same situations. . . .

• Make *moments* in your story. . . . The best way to conceptualize a *moment* is to think of the Emmy Awards. You know those 30 second clips they show when the nominees are read for Best Actress or Best Actor in a series? The clips chosen are invariably *moments*. . . .

• Avoid false jeopardy. Let's be honest: Sometimes you come to a point in the story where the clock indicates you have to have an act break. But there doesn't seem to be any jeopardy around which to structure a break. Some writers just . . . have somebody walk through the door with a gun, however illogical that action might be. Others stop, backtrack, and try to find a thread in the story that can be either moved up or moved back to provide an act curtain. . . .

Have fun with the script. Play with the characters and the situations. Make yourself laugh. If you enjoy the story, you increase the odds substantially that a story editor or producer will feel the same way.

J. MICHAEL STRACZYNSKI *writes scripts for the stage, screen, and radio.*

Connections

Anthology

In "Editing History," the story of a man's life was changed because his government did not approve of his actions. "Retelling Rat Island" by Jamaica Kincaid features a story that is altered for a different reason. Read the account in the *What a Story! Anthology*, and see if you think the change is acceptable.

Many cultures have stories about "shapeshifters," who can change into animals. In "The Hunter and Rainbow Woman," the giant has this characteristic. To read another shapeshifter story with a surprising twist, turn to "The Wife's Story" in the *What a Story! Anthology*.

To follow up on "Ask the Experts," look for more advice on how to craft a story in the *What a Story! Anthology*. The poem "Through that Door" offers an inviting suggestion, while "The Writing of *Shiloh*," "A Writer's Beginning," and "Permission" explain how three writers found inspiration.

Novels

To hear more about storytellers and their influence on listeners, read *The Winter Room* by Gary Paulsen and *A Pack of Lies* by Geraldine McCaughrean. *Paradise Café and Other Stories* by Martha Brooks is a collection of short stories told from the perspective of various teenagers.

Videos

You can hear Wade Hemsworth singing his "Black-Fly Song" on the animated video *Blackfly* in the *What a Story! Video Collection*.

Audiotapes

A story can have different tones or feelings, depending on how you read it. Compare the chilling recitation of Ursula K. Le Guin's "The Wife's Story" with the humorous tone of Saki's "The Story-Teller" on the *What a Story! Audiotape*.

Transparencies

The transparencies that accompany this unit show how twelve artists have attempted to communicate a story visually.

Activities

REREAD "Working for Peanuts," looking for where Schulz's ideas originate. Many of them seem to come from real-life situations Schulz has observed, such as the continual failure of an earnest athlete. This scene appeals to people because they can identify with the feelings that accompany failure. Describe or draw two or more other real-life situations a cartoonist might use to create a humorous story.

PLAY with the borders between fiction and non-fiction. Working from a true story about something that happened to you or to a friend, rearrange the facts so that the story is still believable but is more fun to read than the non-fiction account.

FOLLOW UP on the Express Yourself questions at the end of "The Many Lives of Romeo and Juliet." Use your answers to write a summary of the production you would create. Include a description of the setting, characters, and any plot changes you would make.

FIND another narrative song like "The Black-Fly Song." Many traditional folk songs tell a story, and recently many folk singers have written songs about the environment. Look through books of folk songs or recordings to find a song that uses a story to show concern for the environment. Once you find such a song, think about its effectiveness. How well does the story "work"? Does it persuade you to share the concern of the writer? How?

Co-operative Activity

ENACT A STORY Working in groups of four or five students, tell a story without using words. Each group can choose a simple story (not just a scene!), and decide how to act it out without talking. Observing or reading about mime techniques can help provide ideas for communicating emotions or actions. After all the teams have performed, students can vote on the best performance. Qualities to look for are: which story was most clearly communicated? Which team chose the most interesting and detailed story? Which team used the most creative methods to communicate its story?

THINK of the cartoon of the skier on page 30 as a sort of visual tall tale. Referring to "Tall Tales of Winter" for more ideas, draw your own visual tall tale. Use a story you've heard, or make one up.

Exploring Further

If you enjoy reading folklore, you might look up **Edith Fowke** in the library. She is an award-winning author and collector of Canadian folklore. Fowke has published numerous articles, over twenty books, and several record albums. For a worldwide perspective, try *Favorite Folktales from Around the World,* edited by **Jane Yolen.**

There's more to learn about Charles Schulz in the book *Good Grief: The Story of Charles M. Schulz* by **Rheta Grimsley Johnson.** Johnson covers many aspects of Schulz's life, including his young adulthood and his romance with the real "little red-haired girl."

If you're interested in music, you might explore the ways composers tell stories. Two different approaches are reflected in *Peter and the Wolf* by **Sergei Prokofiev,** which is totally instrumental, and the musical *The Secret Garden* by **Marsha Norman.** Although there are words to portray the story in *The Secret Garden,* composer Lucy Simon has written music which helps tell the story.

Did you read some stories you recognized in "Urban Legends"? To find more, check out some of **Jan Harold Brunvand's** collections of told-as-true tales, such as *The Choking Doberman* or his latest *The Baby Train.*

You can also receive *FOAFtale News* (Friend Of A Friend), the newsletter of the International Society for Contemporary Legend Research, by writing to Bill Ellis, Penn State Hazleton Campus, Hazleton, PA 18201-1291.

The art of storytelling is alive and growing in Canada. One excellent source of information about storytelling groups, concerts, books, tapes, and courses throughout the country is **The Storytellers School of Toronto,** 412-A College Street, Toronto, Ontario, M5T 1T3. Your school might even be able to book a storytelling performance!

Solution to the riddle "The Sticks of Truth" on page 43:

None of the sticks were magical. The only one to worry about being caught, the thief, had cut off two inches of her stick during the night in an effort to hide its growth. But since the sticks were not magical, her stick ended up the only short one.

Credits

A Ligature Book

Photos

Cover © Phillip Singer; **1** © Paul Caulfield/Mirus Films, 22 Rogers Road, Brampton, Ont. L6X 1L8 (t); © James Schnepf (b); © Mary Ditta (r); Photo courtesy of the artist (l); **2** © Eugen Gebhardt/FPG International; **3** © Brilliant/Palmer Photography (b); Provo High School, Provo, Utah (t); **4** © Lambert/Archive Photos (tl); **4–5** © Elizabeth Crews/Stock Boston; **6** © Montreal International Comedy Festival Just For Laughs; **7** © Brilliant/Palmer Photography, Matrioska dolls courtesy of Hannah Grove; **8–9** © Brilliant/Palmer Photography (all); **14–15** © Eugen Gebhardt/FPG International; **20** Photos by John Soares (all); **24–25** Background photography © Brilliant/Palmer Photography; **24** The Bettmann Archive (r); Patrick Roy Hockey Card ®SCORE, 1990; **25** Joe Sakic Hockey Card ®SCORE, 1992; **26** Courtesy of Tololwa Mollel (bl); **28** © Wendy Chan/Gamma-Liaison; **29** Musée de la Reine, Bayeux/The Bridgeman Art Library (b); © David Henderson/Eric Roth Studio (t); **30** Photos provided by Sega of America, Inc. (t); © Brilliant/Palmer Photography (mime); **31** © Axel Poignant Archive (t); **32** Sovfoto; **34** The National Ballet of Canada, C. Von Tiedemann; **35** excerpted from "The Leopold Shakespeare" © Cassell Peter & Galpin; **36** Courtesy of Provo High School, Provo, Utah; **37** Shooting Star; **40** Bill Becker/Canapress (l); **41** © Alex Balych (r); **42** Reproduced by permission of Allan Sapp Paintings Inc.; **44** © David Klutho/Sports Illustrated, Time Inc.

Text

Grateful acknowledgment is given to authors, publishers, and agents for permission to reprint the following copyrighted material. Every effort has been made to determine copyright owners. In the case of any omissions, the Publisher will be pleased to make suitable acknowledgments in future editions.

6 From "A Decade of Laughter" by Christopher Vaughn from *The Hollywood Reporter*, Special Comedy Issue, Volume 323, Number 7. Copyright © 1992 by HR Industries, Inc. Reprinted with permission of *The Hollywood Reporter*.

8 From *The Art of Storytelling: A Guide for Parents, Teachers, Librarians, and Other Storytellers* by Dan Yashinsky. ISBN 0-9693189-0-1. Copyright © 1984 by The Storytellers School of Toronto. Published by The Storytellers School of Toronto, (416) 924-8265.

10 From "If those cobras don't get you, the alligators will" by Richard Wolkomir from *Smithsonian* magazine, November 1992. Reprinted by permission of the author.

13 "Surprise" by Beverly McLoughland originally appeared in *Cricket* magazine, 1985. Reprinted by permission of the author, who controls all rights; "The Story-Teller" from COLLECTED AND NEW POEMS 1924–1963 by Mark Van Doren. Copyright © 1963 by Mark Van Doren. Copyright renewed © 1991 by Dorothy Van Doren. Reprinted by permission of Hill and Wang, a division of Farrar, Straus and Giroux, Inc.

14 From *Earthmaker's Tales* by Gretchen Will Mayo. Copyright © 1989, 1990 by Gretchen Will Mayo. Reprinted by permission from Walker and Company, 720 Fifth Avenue, New York, NY 10019, 1-800-289-2553.

16 From *Good Grief: The Story of Charles M. Schulz* by Rheta Grimsley Johnson. Copyright © 1989 by Pharos Books, a Scripps Howard Company. Reprinted and adapted with permission.

20 From *Faces* December 1991 issue: Storytelling. Copyright © 1991 by Cobblestone Publishing, Inc. 7 School St., Peterborough, NH 03458. Reprinted by permission of the publisher.

23 From *Tall Tales of the Maritimes* by Roland H. Sherwood. Copyright © 1972 by Roland H. Sherwood. Published by Lancelot Press.

26 From "Introducing Tololwa M. Mollel" by Barbara Greenwood from CANSCAIP News, Volume 14, number 1, Spring 1992. Reprinted by permission of the author.

33 From *The Book of Laughter and Forgetting* by Milan Kundera. Copyright © 1980 by Alfred A. Knopf, Inc.

38 "The Black-Fly Song" by Wade Hemsworth. Used by permission of Peermusic Canada, Inc.

40 From "Arctic images provide inspiration in Inuit sculptor's Toronto studio" by Laura Eggertson. Appeared in the *Globe and Mail*, December 29, 1987. Reprinted by permission of The Canadian Press.

41 From *Canadian Geographic* magazine, August/September 1990. Reprinted by permission of the author.

43 From *Stories to Solve: Folktales from Around the World* told by George Shannon. Copyright © 1985 by George W.B. Shannon. By permission of Greenwillow Books, a division of William Morrow & Company, Inc.

44 Reprinted by permission of Grosset & Dunlap. From STRANGE AND INCREDIBLE SPORTS HAPPENINGS by Mac Davis. Copyright © 1975 by Florence Davis.

45 "The TV Commandments" by Michael Straczynski appeared in *Writer's Digest*, April 1992. Reprinted by permission of the author.

Canadian Cataloguing in Publication Data
Main entry under title:

What a Story! : magazine

(MultiSource)
ISBN 0-13-020124-3

1. Storytelling—Literacy collections.   2. Folk literature.
3. Children's literature. I. Iveson, Margaret L., 1948–
II. Robinson, Sam, 1937–   . III. Series

PZ5.W52 1993   j808.83   C92-095391-3